the MiSADVENTURES of

MICHAEL McMICHAELS

The Double-Dog Dare

vol.
4

by **Tony Penn**
illustrated by **Brian Martin**

BOYS TOWN
Press ®

Boys Town, Nebraska

The Misadventures of Michael McMichaels, Vol 4: The Double-Dog Dare
Text and Illustrations Copyright © 2018 by Father Flanagan's Boys' Home
ISBN 978-1-944882-21-1

Published by the Boys Town Press
14100 Crawford St.
Boys Town, NE 68010

For a Boys Town Press catalog, call 1-800-282-6657
or visit our website: BoysTownPress.org

Publisher's Cataloging-in-Publication Data

Names: Penn, Tony, 1973-, author. | Martin, Brian (Brian Michael), 1978-
illustrator.

Title: The misadventures of Michael McMichaels. Vol. 4 : the double-dog dare / by
Tony Penn ; illustrated by Brian Martin.

Other titles: Double-dog dare.

Description: Boys Town, NE : Boys Town Press, [2018] | Audience: grades 3-6.
| Summary: Author Tony Penn has expertly crafted this fourth volume of the
Michael McMichaels series. This time Michael is again choosing inappropriate
behaviors so he can win his friend back from a perceived rival.--Publisher.

Identifiers: ISBN: 978-1-944882-21-1

Subjects: LCSH: Friendship--Juvenile fiction. | Behavior--Juvenile fiction. | Peer
pressure--Juvenile fiction. | Self-esteem--Juvenile fiction. | Interpersonal
relations in children--Juvenile fiction. | Interpersonal communication in
children--Juvenile fiction. | Children--Life skills guides. | CYAC: Friendship-
-Fiction. | Behavior--Fiction. | Peer pressure--Fiction. | Self-esteem-- Fiction.
| Interpersonal communication--Fiction. | Interpersonal relations--Fiction. |
Conduct of life. | BISAC: JUVENILE FICTION / Readers / Chapter Books. |
JUVENILE FICTION / Social Themes / Friendship. | JUVENILE FICTION
/ Social Themes / Peer Pressure. | JUVENILE FICTION / Social Themes /
Emotions & Feelings. | JUVENILE NONFICTION / Social Topics / Friendship.

Classification: LCC: PZ7.1.P456 M4724 2018 | DDC: [Fic]--dc23

Boys Town Press is the publishing division of
Boys Town, a national organization serving
children and families.

10 9 8 7 6 5 4 3 2 1

For Michael, Patricia,
Christopher, and Matthew

Chapter 1

You're not going to believe **THE MESS** **I got myself into this time.** My life stinks! It stinks worse than garbage just before you're about to walk it to the curb. Have you ever leaned in and sniffed it then? I suggest you don't, especially if there's a baby's diaper in there. In that case, I'd hold the garbage with one hand and pinch my nostrils with the other. (You'll need someone to open the front door for you if you do that, but you get the point.)

Well, I'd rather stick my face in the garbage for an hour than have to deal with the mess I got myself into this time. It's a Double-Dog Dare contest with a really crazy rich kid, Zeke, who threatened to give me a HUGE dare! Something he said he KNEW I'd be too chicken to do. And, it's bad, REALLY bad. But I have to do it because if I don't, it means I'm not really my buddy Kenny's best friend. Before I tell you what it is, I need to let you know how all of this started.

You see, it started as kind of fun, but now it's gotten out of hand, and I don't know how to stop it. Why does this kind of thing always happen to me?

Everything was going fine and dandy until a couple of weeks ago when Kenny had his birthday party. It was a normal kind of party at his house with kids from our class and the neighborhood who went to different schools. There was also a clown, but I couldn't wait for him to finish up because I find clowns annoying.

We ate lasagna, played some fun games and were at the gift-giving part when the "incident" happened. Just to be polite, everyone was oohing and aahing at every gift, the way people do. Even the socks, Absimil, a new student in our class

2

from Somalia, got for Kenny impressed everyone. Absimil and his family were living with another family in our area because they were refugees. We all knew they didn't have much money but, really, who wants to get socks for a gift? There were also a couple of video-game gifts, which the kids seemed the most excited about. And, from me, a boxed set of *Encyclopedia Brown* books because I know Kenny likes to read, and I couldn't bear my best friend not knowing about my favorite series any longer.

So far, so good, right? Well, up until another new kid in the school, Zeke, handed Kenny his gift, everything was fine. Zeke had moved to the area a few weeks ago, into the biggest and most expensive house that an old doctor and his wife had lived in since before I was born. Zeke's parents work for some fancy company, and not only are they rich, they want everyone to know it. They already added an extra floor and a pool to the house they bought. Zeke's dad's car is red, foreign, and shiny. His mother wears sparkly jewelry and fancy clothes like ladies at a wedding. Zeke is also in Ms. Mitchell's class with Kenny and me, and lots of kids find him annoying because he's always asking how much everyone's sneakers cost and where they went on their last vacation, etc., to try to find out how much money they have.

Kenny recently started talking to Zeke about basketball, which I don't know much about because it just seems like a bunch of guys running back and forth and making squeaking noises with their sneakers. Since Kenny's parents drive an expensive car, I guess Zeke found him fancy enough to be friends with because Kenny invited him to the party. Right after Kenny opened my gift, he opened Zeke's. It was a tower of video games, and when I say tower, **I mean a TOWER!** It was at least as high as Kenny himself, and the other kids in the room started freaking out when they saw it. Everyone looked at Zeke like he was in a movie or knew Ellen DeGeneres personally or something. I felt like such an idiot for getting Kenny a measly set of five paperback books, but you know what? Looking around the room, I could tell that everyone else felt the same way about their gifts. Who could compete with a tower of video games?

That's when I decided to take matters into my

own hands. After the fuss of the fancy gift died down, and Kenny's mother brought out the cupcakes (which always make you happy for a few minutes, let's face it), I sprang into action. Zeke was in the corner by himself texting his parents. He was my height, had wavy blond hair, skinny legs like a frog, and one of those butt chins that

give me funny feelings. I reached out and covered the screen of his phone with my hand, then screwed up my eyes like actors on TV do when they are mad.

"Hey, what's going on?" Zeke asked.

"What's going on," I said, "is that you made us all look cheap and stupid with that crazy gift of yours."

"Oh, really? You asked everyone? You're speaking for them?" he said, looking all rich and confident.

"I can just tell. I don't need to talk to them," I answered.

"Listen, kid, just because you gave him a cheap set of books, doesn't mean it's my fault," Zeke said. "Who cares about books anymore, really?"

"Smart people do, that's who," I said. "And what do you think that tower of junk proves anyway? Do you think it means you're a better friend to Kenny than I am?"

He didn't even hesitate to reply.

"Yes, I know it does," he said. "Because Kenny just told me I'm his new best friend."

"He told you WHAT?" I asked.

"You heard me," Zeke said confidently.

"I did, you're right. I'm standing really close to you and I have perfect hearing," I said. "But I'm not going to accept it. Kenny and I have been friends since you and your family lived in that bank, or wherever you're originally from, and it's going to take more than a stack of video games to change that."

"A tower. It's a **TOWER**, not a stack," Zeke bragged.

"Fine, tower, whatever," I said.

"So, hotshot, if you think you're really Kenny's best friend, I dare you to stand on that table and cluck like a chicken," Zeke said, like he'd been planning that all afternoon or something.

I was really nervous at that point, but I didn't want moneybags to know it, so I played it cool. "Sure, no big deal. Watch and weep..." I said, walking over to the table and whistling as if what I was about to do was normal.

And then I did it. I hopped on Kenny's dining room table and began to cluck like a chicken.

"Bawk, bawk, bawk, bawk, bawk..." I flapped

my arms and moved my head back and forth. I have to admit I felt very chickeny.

The kids began to gather around the table and laugh and so did Kenny's parents. But they also told me to get down because they didn't want me to fall.

Kenny's father reached out for me, and as I was in mid-air, heading toward the floor, I stuck out my tongue at Zeke, who looked worried. He knew I'd dare him to do something next.

"So, big deal, you can hop on a table and cluck like a chicken," he said nervously.

"You **dared** me to, and I did it! Now it's my turn," I said. "If you think you're really Kenny's **best friend,**

I double-dog dare you to... to..."

I couldn't think of anything. Really. Not a thing.

"Ha! Loser. You can't even think of a good dare. They come so easily to me," Zeke said.

"Yeah, because you're EVIL. Wait a second. I've got it!" I said, rubbing my chin.

"So, ah, what is it?" Zeke asked, beginning to shake. "Remember, Double-Dog Dare rules are it can't hurt anyone, and no matter how many dares there are, it's always called a double-dog dare because triple-dog dare and quadruple-dog dare don't sound as good, ok?"

The kid had a point.

"Sure, fine. I don't want to see blood," I said. "I just want you to admit that I'm Kenny's best friend."

"Only if I can't do the dare or refuse to try," Zeke said. "That's how it works, so spit it out. I'm ready."

"Take it easy. I'll tell you in school tomorrow," I said.

"Fine," Zeke said. And we both headed home.

Chapter 2

On the bus to school the next day I sat next to Kenny, as usual.

"Kenny," I said while he was yawning, "let's say you were going to dare a kid in our class to do something, what would it be?"

"Why would I do that?" Kenny said.

"Let's just say you're playing a game, ok?" I replied.

"Mikey, I don't like the sound of this," Kenny said, looking concerned. "I feel like you're going to get us in trouble again with another one of your crazy ideas."

"Who said anything about crazy ideas? I just need a good idea for a dare," I explained.

"Well, you never call them crazy ideas, but in

11

the end, that's what they turn out to be," Kenny said. "You're going to make me need an inhaler or a paper bag to breathe into or something. I get anxiety when you get these ideas of yours."

"Trust me," I said, looking into his eyes, "as your **BEST FRIEND**, trust me." I was waiting to see if he corrected me and said that Zeke was his new best friend, but he didn't flinch or say anything.

"Ok then, my idea for a double-dog dare would be to tell the kid to repeat everything Harriet says all day today," Kenny said. "It's really annoying when people do that."

"Thanks! You're a genius," I said. "You can go back to sleep now. I'll wake you up when we're at school."

I loved the idea.

In class, before we began our first activity of the day, I walked up to Zeke and whispered in his ear: "Hey, so here's my double-dog dare."

"It better be good," he said, "took you long enough."

"Oh, it's good," I said.

"I double-dog dare you to repeat everything Harriet says all day today."

"Big deal! I can handle that," he said.

"We'll see about that," I said, and returned to my seat.

An hour or so went by without Harriet raising her hand or being called on, so I started to get nervous that my dare wasn't that good. But then Ms. Mitchell asked the class if anyone knew what the word "dissuade" meant. Harriet's arm shot straight up.

"It means to discourage someone from doing something, Ms. Mitchell."

"Can you use it in a sentence, Harriet?" Ms. Mitchell asked.

"Yes, I can," she said, standing up and smiling as she always does when she gives an answer. She can be so annoying! "I tried to dissuade my little brother from eating the rest of the cake, but he did it anyway."

"Excellent example, Harriet," Ms. Mitchell said.

I looked over at Zeke and thought I had won the dare because I couldn't hear anything coming from his mouth, but then I saw his lips moving. **DARN IT!** He was repeating everything Harriet was saying, only in a whisper. I never said he had to say it out loud. **UGH!** He's a clever one, that kid.

I got really depressed that I would lose the bet and that would mean Kenny is not my best friend anymore, so I sighed and glanced down at the floor. I could see that my sneakers were pretty old and weren't a fancy brand. They were just sneakers, and I was fine with them until I looked over at Zeke's and saw his were new, perfect, and expensive. Until recently, I didn't spend much time thinking about fancy things and who is rich and who is not, but Zeke, with all of his family's money, and Absimil, whose family is very poor, have made me wonder about it a lot. I don't know why some people have so much and some people have so little. I'm glad I have a house and food and a family, but Zeke is really making me jealous. Come to think of it, my house seems smaller to me all of a sudden and my clothes seem ratty. I want perfect, shiny sneakers, too. Anyway, how can anyone keep their sneakers that perfect? I was curious so I asked him after school.

"Hey, Zeke. So, you won that double-dog dare, fine," I said.

"Pretty slick, right? I just whispered every time she spoke. The kid next to me thought I was crazy, but whatever. I won!"

"I know, I said that already. What I want to

know is how do you keep your sneakers so perfect? I mean, they look brand new," I asked.

"Because they ARE brand new," he said. "I have tons and tons of pairs, and I wear a different pair every day. They never look old because they never are."

"Oh," I said, looking down again at mine. "That's a lot of new sneakers."

"My parents are RICH, so that's why," Zeke said.

"I can see, for sure. Anyway, time for your next double-dog dare. And I can do it, I'm ready," I said, but, really, I was super nervous.

"Ok, you know that old abandoned house at the end of the cul-de-sac?" he asked.

"Ah, yeah, the one that everyone says is haunted?" I said, nervously.

"Yep. I double-dog dare you to bring me back the gold ring that's in the basement," he said.

"Wait, WHAT?" I asked. "Have you been watching the movie, *Lord of the Rings?*"

"Yes, I have, and so what?" Zeke answered.

"I left a gold ring in the basement, and you have to bring it back to me at my house tonight or that means that I'm really Kenny's best friend."

"Is the ring real gold?" I asked, remembering the Borrowed Bracelet, not wanting to get myself into trouble again.

"Of course it's real! I'm RICH, I told you!" he said.

"And is it YOURS? I don't want to take someone else's property," I said.

Zeke seemed annoyed. "Of course it's mine! I'm no thief."

"Ok, fine," I said confidently. "I will return your ring from Mordor – I mean that haunted house – tonight, because I can do it, and I am really Kenny's best friend."

"We'll see about that tomorrow," he said with a laugh.

"Yes, we will!" I said.

Chapter 3

At home, I didn't realize how nervous I was about getting the ring from that haunted **house down the block.** But my mother noticed my glass of milk was shaking as I lifted it to my mouth. She noticed because the milk was spilling over the top of the glass! (I always have a glass of milk and just one cookie after school. It's a small thing, but I look forward to it. It's important to have something small to look forward to, I think.)

"Michael, what's the matter? You're shaking. Are you nervous about something?" she asked from across the kitchen.

I knew I had to say something, so I blurted out the first thing that came to mind.

"Yeah, uh, Ms. Mitchell talked to us about volcanoes today, and she said there's a town in Italy called Bombay and it was buried after a volcano exploded," I said. "What if that happens to us? I don't want to be buried in lava."

"Michael, no one does, and you don't need to worry because there are no volcanoes anywhere near us," Mom said. "Besides, that town in Italy is called Pompeii, not Bombay."

"Ok, phew," I said, but, apparently, she wasn't convinced.

"What's the real problem?" she said. "Tell me. I know you like the back of my hand."

I had never heard that expression before, but then I looked at the back of my hand, and I got it and smiled. Still, I couldn't tell her what was really going on, so I had to think quickly.

"I was actually wondering about astronauts," I said.

"Astronauts?" she said, taking the seat next to me at the kitchen table. I had just finished my cookie and was wishing there was another one there. (I always wish there was more dessert, don't you?)

"Yeah, I was wondering how they go to the bathroom in space," I said. "My teacher said there's no gravity up there so where does it..."

She stopped me right there. "Ok, enough of this," she blurted out. "Young man, tell me immediately what is going on!"

"All right, all right," I said. "I'm just worried that Kenny is impressed by this new rich kid, Zeke, and that he's going to become his new best friend."

It actually felt better to tell her that much. For one, it wasn't a lie, but, of course, it wasn't the whole truth. The whole truth is something I'm not very good at, but I'm trying.

"Well, that's more like it," she said. "Finally, the truth. Listen, sweetie, you and Kenny have been best friends for years and Zeke may become a new friend of his, but I have a feeling your bond with Kenny goes very deep. I mean, think of all the trouble you two have gotten into together!"

"True, Mom, thanks," I said, relieved.

Then she hugged me, and I went to my room. I plopped onto my bed and just wanted to sleep, but I could see the sun setting so I knew I had to act fast to get the ring from that haunted house.

I called Kenny and asked him if he could meet me in front of my house right away. I was glad he said yes.

"What's up?" he asked on my front lawn.

"Oh, nothing, I just wanted to take a walk," I said. "It's a beautiful night, right?"

"Why do you have that flashlight in your hand?" Kenny asked.

"No reason. Well, the sun's setting now, and you have to be prepared." I was trying to be convincing.

We started to walk in the direction of that abandoned house at the end of the cul-de-sac.

"I smell a problem," Kenny said. "You're up to something."

"I mean, I may want to do something small, you know, but nothing you can't handle," I replied.

"That's it," Kenny said. "I need an inhaler or a paper bag to breathe into. I'm getting **NERVOUS**, Mikey."

"Don't worry. It'll be ok," I said.

We approached the abandoned house at the

end of the cul-de-sac, and I told him I just wanted to go exploring a bit, that we never know what may be in there, maybe even treasure! Kenny said that was crazy, but he did walk with me to the front porch of that big, old, sad-looking house with its paint peeling off and cobwebs everywhere.

My heart was pounding in my chest and Kenny was hyperventilating, but I did it – I rang the bell.

No one answered.

"Ok, that's it. No one's home. It's over. Back home for us!" Kenny said, turning around.

"Wait, I hear footsteps!" I said.

Just then a small bird flew over our heads.

"**Call 911! Call the FBI! Call Ellen!**" I cried.

"**UUUUGHHHHH!** We're dead. **It's over,**" Kenny screamed and collapsed.

Kenny had fainted, but there was no time to help him. I was on my own. I glanced up at the open door and saw… Zeke and his parents and some guy with a pencil over his ear.

"Hey, you're Michael, right?" Zeke's mother said. "Zeke told us to expect you."

24

"Oh, ok," I said with my hand on my chest. I thought I was going to have a heart attack.

"What's the matter? Are you boys ok? Why is Kenny sleeping on the porch?" Zeke's mother said.

I could see Zeke cracking up behind his mother.

"Oh, Kenny's not sleeping," I said. "He fainted because we, ah… saw a bat. Yeah, a bat."

"A bat!" his mother said, surprised.

"Yeah, not a baseball bat, I mean the scary ones that fly," I said.

"I know, how terrible!" she said.

Kenny got up. We gave him a bottle of water, and he was fine. It turned out that Zeke's parents had bought that old abandoned house and were planning to make it all new and fancy. That's why that guy with the pencil over his ear was there. He was a contractor. Zeke's father said they were going to "flip the house."

"Flip it?" I asked. "Isn't it kind of heavy for that?"

"No," his father said, laughing. "That means we'll fix it up and sell it soon for a much higher price and make a lot of money."

"Oh," I said, "gotcha!" And I decided that that was enough.

Kenny and I said goodbye to Zeke, his parents, and that guy with the pencil over his ear, then we began to walk home.

"You nearly killed me this time!" Kenny said.

"I know. I kind of thought you were dead there for a second, but I could see your chest going up and down so I knew you were alive," I said.

"Thanks a lot. No more walks up the block with you! I need to get home and do my homework," Kenny said.

"You're mad?" I asked.

"YES! I fainted because I thought ghosts or crazy people were going to come out of that house and kill us," Kenny said. "Who WOULDN'T be mad?"

"Ok, good point, but you're still my friend?" I said, hoping he would forgive me... AGAIN!

"Yes! But you need to stop with these crazy adventures because I'm going to wind up in the nervous hospital if you continue," he said.

"Ok, ok, I'll stop," I said.

Then he went home, but a part of me didn't believe him. A part of me thought he would really become best friends with Zeke because he could flip a house. All I could do is get us into trouble. I think I need an inhaler or a paper bag myself!

As I was heading down the sidewalk to my house, I felt a tap on my shoulder. It was Zeke.

"That was hilarious," he said, laughing.

"Ok, but I won that round because I tried to get the ring," I said.

"Yes, you did, you did," he said, still cracking up. Then he looked at me all serious and said that his family was now so rich that they were going to buy MY house soon. He laughed an evil laugh then ran back down the street to his house — or should I say houses?

Chapter 4

When I got home I noticed my heart was beating super fast. I was really nervous thinking that Zeke's rich parents would buy our house, but also because I thought I had finally gone too far and been too much for Kenny to handle. He would drop me as a best friend for sure. I probably wouldn't even make his top 100! I went into the bathroom to splash my face with cold water to calm down. I'd known Kenny since I was born (he's a month older than me) and we've been best friends ever since. Well, we weren't really friends when we were teeny tiny babies because you can't talk – or even walk – then, but I think you get the point.

As I walked out of the bathroom with my face

dripping cold water, I bumped into my brother, Joey.

"Hey, Joe," I said.

"Hey, why is your face wet? Did you fall into the toilet?" he asked, giggling.

"No, I...I...," I had no idea what to say.

"What were you doing in there, bobbing for apples in the toilet?" He dropped to the floor because he thought he was hilarious. I hate when people laugh at their own jokes!

I didn't even bother to answer him because I knew he wouldn't care or understand. Instead, I went into the living room to see what was on TV. I was going through the stations with the remote when I saw the beginning of one of those animal documentaries on cable. It was about lions in Africa. I thought about Absimil right away and wondered if he ever saw a lion when he lived there. I decided I would ask him about Somalia the next chance I got because I never heard anything about it and never even saw any pictures.

The documentary was really interesting because these lions have very simple lives. When they aren't eating, sleeping, or catching something to eat, they kind of just lounge around, rolling in the grass, just chilling. I decided I wanted to be a lion (except for the part about being naked all the time – gross!) because being a human is sometimes too hard.

But guess what? It turns out lions sometimes have difficult lives, too. The documentary showed

two lion cub buddies, wandering off, playing in the grass. They traveled a bit too far from the other lions, but everything was going well until another lion cub their age from a nearby jungle approached them and started playing with only one of the old-friend cubs. They totally ignored the other cub and eventually he wound up trying to get back to the other lions. But he couldn't find his way and got lost. The program ended with him roaming around the tall grass of Africa, which is long and swaying and beautiful and not all short and mowed like our grass.

What happened to that lost cub? I wondered as I watched all the names of the people who made the TV show go on and on and on.

I was so sad thinking about the lion cub losing his friend to that new lion cub – and maybe even dying out there all alone in the grass – that I got really sad.

Just then my little sister Abby walked into the room.

"What's the matter, Michael?" she said with her head tilted a bit sideways. I could tell she really cared, so I told her.

"I'm scared that Kenny doesn't want to be my friend anymore," I said.

"Why?" she asked

"Because that new rich kid, Zeke, bought him a big expensive present for his birthday, and he's a lot fancier than we are," I explained.

"Kenny's your friend, silly," Abby said.

"I know, I just don't know if he will still want to be," I said.

"He will," she said confidently.

"How do you know that?" I asked.

"I don't know," she said, and walked up to me and hugged me. It kind of sounds corny, but that hug made me feel really good.

Later that night as I was in bed, waiting to fall asleep, I started to think of a double-dog dare for Zeke. It took me a while, but I had the best idea and it involved Harriet again!

I was sure this dare would be so difficult for Zeke to do that he'd refuse to even try. Then I'd win and could say, finally, that Kenny is my best friend and close that subject forever!

Chapter 5

On the bus on the way to school the next day I sat next to Kenny, as usual. I felt the need to make him laugh so I decided to tell him a joke.

"Kenny, what kind of dinosaur knew the most words?" I asked.

"Huh?" He looked at me, surprised.

"The The-SAUR-us!" I said, blurting out the answer.

"What? Oh. Ha! That's funny," he said.

"I have one more," I told him.

"Ok, let's hear," he said.

I felt better already because he was smiling and liked my first joke.

"What do you call a sleeping dinosaur?" I asked.

"Ah… ah… I don't know," he said. "Wait! A dino-snore!"

"Yes!" I said.

Then we high-fived and went into the school to start the day. I was really glad Kenny was smiling, but I knew I had to find Zeke to tell him what the next double-dog dare would be.

Sure enough, he came up to me by the coat hooks. He was laughing.

"That was so funny, last night," he said. "You two were SO scared!"

"Yeah, yeah," I said. "Next subject."

"No, I'm not done with that subject. Did you pee your pants? Did Kenny?" Zeke asked, still cracking up.

"All right, fine, I did, maybe a little bit. You happy now?" I asked.

"Yes!" Zeke said.

"So now it's my turn give you your next double-dog dare, and this one is really good. You're not going to be able to do it, and I'm going to win," I said.

"Ok, I'm ready, let's hear," Zeke was wiping the tears from his cheeks from laughing really hard.

"I dare you to propose to Harriet, right after her presentation today," I said.

"Propose?" Zeke asked, looking confused.

"Yeah, ask her to marry you, in front of the whole class," I said.

"Hmmmm," Zeke said, rubbing his chin. "The only problem with that is we said the dares can't harm anyone."

"How is proposing to her harming her?" I asked.

"Well, maybe it will hurt her feelings," Zeke said.

"Harriet? Feelings? Ha! Don't worry, she'll be fine," I said. "And anyway, it's a compliment if someone wants to marry you."

"I guess you're right," Zeke said. "But we're too young to get married," he pointed out.

"I KNOW! You don't have to actually marry her," I said. "Just propose on your knee in front of

37

the whole class."

"Ok, fine. I accept the dare," Zeke said. "Right after her presentation today?"

"Yes!" I responded, confident that this would be the dare that wins me the competition.

We each had to do a presentation on a topic we recently studied. The other day I presented about cheetahs, and I was a big hit because I gave everyone in the class, including Ms. Mitchell, a bag of Cheetos. People are always happy when you feed them, I've noticed.

Two of us had to present each day. Today it was Absimil's and Harriet's turn.

When Absimil was presenting about the planet Jupiter, I wasn't really paying attention much because I kept staring at him trying to imagine Somalia. I wondered if everyone there looked like him. He had such a unique face: His nose was really tiny and his eyes were the shape of pecans in their shell, like the ones my father eats after dinner. I repeated Somalia over and over in my head. Were there lions and tigers and cheetahs there? What exactly is a refugee? What language does he speak to his parents and sister? I heard them in the lobby a few days ago, and it sounded really nice except I couldn't understand a word of it. It must be difficult to move to another country when you're a kid. I wonder if he misses Somalia. I'll bet he still has friends there that he misses a lot. Maybe he even has a best friend. I wonder if he has someone like Kenny who he misses. I decided I would sit next to Absimil in the cafeteria soon and strike up a conversation to see what I could find out.

After Absimil finished, Harriet took to the stage. Ugh. Here we go. She's going to be perfect again and get a 100 on her presentation.

Harriet presented on Marie Curie, who was a Polish-French scientist. She was dressed as a scientist and even brought in a chemistry set so she could act out a skit as Marie Curie.

Harriet poured some blue liquid into a jar, stirred it and said in her annoying English accent, "I have poured this liquid into this jar because I am a genius scientist and that is what we do."

She stirred it again.

"Presto! I have discovered radioactivity!" Harriet cried out.

"Now, I shall be the first woman to win the Nobel prize. And because I am such a genius, I will win it TWICE! The only person to EVER do that!" she said, pointing to the board where a giant number **2** was flashing over and over again.

The class clapped, and in her lab coat and thick scientist-glasses, Harriet took a bow.

I looked over at Zeke who was rolling up a piece of paper. I wondered what he was up to. He's kind of unpredictable, that kid.

Harriet was smiling at her accomplishment when all of a sudden Zeke raised his hand.

"Zeke, do you have a question about Marie Curie? I'd be happy to answer," Harriet said.

"Well, I have a question," he said, approaching Harriet. "But it's not about Marie Curie." Then he started to giggle and, reaching out a little paper ring that he had just made, asked her to marry him, only it was very hard to hear him because he was giggling so much.

"Marry YOU! Are you crazy?"

Harriet screamed. She was **FUMING.**

"I am going to marry Prince Harry, not some vulgar child like you who wears new clothing from the mall every day! Ms. Mitchell, did you hear what he said to me? Do something, please, do something!"

Ms. Mitchell had already called the principal's office because a minute later Principal Stein arrived and asked Zeke to go with him to his office.

I kind of felt bad for Harriet. She began to cry and put her head down on the desk. Ms. Mitchell gave her a pass to the bathroom so she could "compose" herself.

I was mad at myself for not realizing the dare might hurt Harriet's feelings. She's annoying, but just because some people are annoying doesn't mean they don't have feelings, right? This is another mess I got myself into.

Except it wasn't over yet. Because Zeke completed the double-dog dare, he'd dare me to do something again. But what could it be? There are so many things he can ask me to do, and I'm scared that I won't have the guts like he did to do what he says. It's getting serious now.

Maybe I should just consider dropping out of this little game after all? But then that would mean Zeke wins and he'd be Kenny's new best friend. On the way to the bus that afternoon, Zeke ran to catch up to me in the school's parking lot.

"So, I did it," he said, smiling.

"You did, I know. Did you get in trouble?" I asked.

"Yeah, the principal called my father," Zeke said. "But he was in a meeting, so he called my mother, but she was in a meeting, too."

"Think you'll get punished?" I asked.

"Probably not," he answered. "My parents work a lot so they don't really have time for stuff like that."

"Wow," I said. My parents always found time to punish me if I did a bad thing. I guess I should be grateful. I kind of felt bad for him for a second there.

It was just a second, though, because then, just as I was about to get into the bus, Zeke made an evil face and said he was ready to tell me what my next double-dog dare was.

"Ok," I said, "I'm ready."

He leaned in so no one near us could hear and said, "I double-dog dare you to call Absimil poor."

"What?" I cried. I was shocked.

"You heard me. Call him poor," Zeke said in

his evil tone.

"Why would I do that?" I asked.

"Because THAT is what I'm double-dog daring you to do, and if you can't do it, that means I'm really Kenny's best friend," Zeke said.

"What a crazy thing to say. Where did you get that idea from anyway?" I asked.

"Look at his clothes, that's how," Zeke said. "And, besides, he's a refugee and refugees are poor people from other countries."

"I guess you're right," I said.

"You think you have the guts to do it?" Zeke asked. "Or are you chicken?"

"I guess I can do it," I said. "But won't it hurt him if I ask that? Didn't you say that was a rule of the game?"

"Yeah, but you asked me to propose to Harriet and that wasn't so nice," Zeke reminded me. "So I can ask you this, right?"

"Ok," I said, but I had a very bad feeling about this one. Considering how hard this dare was, I told Zeke I should get a week to do it. At first, he said no, but finally he agreed. That gave me some time to think about this more and also some time to get to know Absimil better.

Remember I told you earlier how my life stinks worse than garbage just before you're about to walk it to the curb? Well, I really wasn't kidding. I'm here at home trying to concentrate on my homework, but it's impossible. All I can think about is hurting Absimil's feelings by saying he's poor.

What should I do?

Chapter 6

Later that day, I began to imagine Zeke and his parents buying our house. Where would we live? They are so rich that they could afford to buy and even "flip" our house.

I began to panic. What could I do to help my family? I ran to check my wallet and found $4.65. How much do houses cost anyway?

I had to get creative.

I know! I can start a charity and ask the neighbors for their support. I can have a bake sale or do tons of other things to raise enough money.

Abby and I just finished our milk and cookies when I told her to come with me. I grabbed a plastic bag and we told our mother we'd be back soon, that we were taking a walk. I couldn't tell my mother the truth, right? She'd be furious! But I knew I was doing the right thing because I was trying to save my family from losing our house and even being homeless!

We went from door to door, straight down the block. I know all of my neighbors on my side of the street, so it was kind of easy. I just said we were collecting for "poor people" and in no time, I had $40!

At one house, there was an old man, Mr. Jacobs, who lived by himself. He walked with a cane and it took him **FOREVER** to answer the front door.

"Hello there, McMichaels children!" he said.

"Hey, Mr. Jacobs," I said, and I began to feel bad about what I was doing. But then I thought, I'm not lying if I say we're collecting for poor people because next to Zeke we are poor, right? Something inside me knew I was making a mistake, but I chose to ignore that because I was really scared of losing our house.

"What can I help you with?" he asked.

"We're, uh, collecting for the poor," I said.

"Oh, that's so very nice of you, Michael," he said. Then he gave me $5.

"Thanks, Mr. Jacobs," I said. "Can I ask you a question?"

"Of course you can, Michael," he answered.

"Have you noticed that new rich family down the block with their fancy cars and clothes?" I asked.

"Yes," he said, laughing.   "Yes, I have."

"Why are you laughing?" I asked.

"Because they are putting on a show, only no one is watching," Mr. Jacobs said.

"A show?" I asked.

"Yes. Those clothes and cars are meant to impress us," he explained. "It's all very silly, really. It's better to be humble and modest like your family."

"Thanks, Mr. Jacobs," I said.

"Thanks, Mr. Jacobs," Abby chimed in, too. I had kind of forgotten she was there while he was talking because I was really interested in what he was saying.

Maybe he's right. Maybe they are just silly people, and I shouldn't take them seriously. But everyone 'oohs' and 'aahs' at their money, so that must mean they are important. If Mr. Jacobs says it's better to be humble and honest, then why don't people 'ooh' and 'aah' at that?

I thought about these things as Abby and I headed back home.

When I got to my room, I put the money in my sock drawer and went downstairs for dinner with my family.

"What's for dinner, Ma?" I asked.

"Pasta with broccoli," she answered.

"I love that!" I said.

We all started to eat and then my father asked us if we'd want to go to the county fair that Saturday.

All at once, Joey, Abby, and I screamed, "YES!"

"What do they have there, Daddy?" Abby asked.

"There are rides and games and concerts and plenty of food and drink," he said.

"Sounds great!" I said.

"Yeah," Joey said. "And my teacher even told us today that there is a contest with a big prize at the end of the night. I think something like $200."

When he said that, I knew what I had to do: I had to win that contest and give the money to my parents so Zeke's family wouldn't buy our house.

I could even invite Absimil! I'm sure he'd have a great time. I wonder if he's even seen a roller coaster before.

That night, I had trouble falling asleep because I was so anxious about so many things. But, finally, I fell asleep and had the worst dream ever. I dreamed that Zeke's family bought our house and we were homeless.

My family and I had to wander around in our underwear because we were so poor we couldn't even afford clothes. Eventually, we wound up in Africa and were walking in the tall wild grass, and it was beautiful. The sun seemed so much bigger than it did back home. The air was clear and it felt great to breathe. I looked down, and I was wearing my purple underwear with green polka dots, but it didn't really matter because the grass went all the way up to my chest.

Then I remembered the lions in that nature

special I saw on TV.

"LIONS!" I screamed and we all began to run, but it turned out there weren't any lions. Then, in the distance, we saw giant – I mean ENORMOUS – brand-new sneakers, the size of giraffes, which were expensive and shiny. They were everywhere and they were coming toward us.

"Run!" I screamed, as my family and I ran in our

UNDERWEAR.

But the sneakers were so big and going so fast, soon they caught up and surrounded us.

Then Zeke and his parents popped up from inside one of the sneakers. They were wearing gold clothes and big diamond hats.

My family and I huddled together.

"What do you want with us?" my mother cried. "You already bought our house. Leave us alone! We're trying to get away from you!"

"We want everything!" they said.

"We are greedy and we won't be happy until we have **EVERYTHING, EVERYTHING, EVERYTHING,**" they kept repeating as they reached out their hands and tried to grab us!

Just then I woke up. It was 3 o'clock in the morning, and I was breathing and sweating like I just ran a marathon. But I was glad the dream was over. You ever have a terrible dream and wake up scared in the middle of the night? Well, it's not fun.

Finally, I fell asleep. The next morning, I was excited because I would sit next to Absimil in the cafeteria and would ask him if he wanted to come to the county fair with us.

I tried to forget about Zeke's double-dog dare and having to call Absimil poor, but it wasn't easy.

Why did I agree to this crazy Double-Dog Dare contest anyway?

Chapter 7

During lunch, Absimil was sitting next to a **couple of quiet kids** in our class, a few tables away from where Kenny and I usually sit.

"Hey, is that space free?" I asked, pointing to the space across from him.

"Yes," Absimil said. He was eating the peanut butter and jelly sandwich that is the sort of backup meal the cafeteria always serves.

"You don't like ham?" I said, sitting down.

"I can't eat ham because of my religion," he said. I liked the way he said the words. He had an interesting accent and he kind of had to pause between each word to think about the next one. I was jealous because I couldn't speak any languages except English.

"What's your religion?" I asked.

"I am Muslim," Absimil said.

"Oh, ok. Wait a second," I said. "My neighbor, Mr. Jacobs, is Jewish and he can't have ham either. I guess your religions are kind of the same, right?"

"Well, they are, a bit," Absimil said. "But they are different. Do you have a religion?"

"I'm Catholic," I replied. "We can eat anything. I think. Actually, I don't really know because sometimes I don't pay attention in religion class."

Absimil smiled. "I know, sometime class is boring, right?"

"It's SO true!" I said.

I glanced down to see what kind of sneakers he was wearing. They were even older than mine, and I wondered if he was jealous of Zeke's new sneakers every day, too.

Just then, Harriet walked by us with her lunch tray. She looked down her nose at me and I made a face back at her. Then, all of a sudden, she tripped, screamed **"OH NO!"** and fell to the ground. Her food went everywhere, and the whole cafeteria went silent for a second.

I started to laugh.

Absimil jumped up, ran around the table, and helped her up. She was covered in milk, pears, and corn. Her slice of pizza was on the floor, face-down, right near her leg.

"Thank you," she said, as Absimil helped her to her feet. "And don't anyone take photos of me now and sell them to the paparazzi, ok? If Prince Harry sees this, I am done for. He will NEVER want to marry me then!"

Absimil sat back down next to me like nothing happened and began eating again.

"Serves her right," I said. "She thinks she's the

best with her English accent and her 100 on every test. I think she deserved that because she made fun of my 85 on the math test we got back this morning."

"She does not deserve to fall. No one deserves to fall," Absimil said.

I felt terrible. I guess he was right. Harriet is a loony tune, for sure, but she doesn't deserve to fall and get covered by three different food groups.

I asked Absimil if he would like to join me and my family at the county fair on Saturday. He didn't know what a county fair was, and I had to explain it. In fact, I even had to draw a roller coaster and a Ferris wheel on a napkin so he would know what I was talking about. Once he realized what I meant, he smiled and said, "Yes! It's like I see in movies on TV in Somalia. We not have that there, but I love to go. Thank you, Michael. But I ask my mother and father first." He said 'motha' and 'fatha,' and sometimes left words out of his sentences. I loved the way it sounded.

After I did my homework that afternoon, I started to get nervous again about Zeke's family buying our house. I decided it would send a message to him if I would stand guard at our front door like the soldiers do in front of the White House. Then I realized I'm not a soldier, and I'm only in the third grade. What could I do in case they show up with their buckets of money and decide to buy our house right out from under us?

I got it! I needed to build a fort for protection. I called Kenny and he came over right away.

"What's going on now, Mikey?" Kenny asked.

"Nothing," I said. "Well, we need to build a fort so Zeke can't get in and buy my house."

"Buy your house? WHAT?" he asked.

"You heard me. His parents are rich acrobats or flippers or something," I said. "They are going to buy all the houses on the block, including YOURS, and flip them. We have to build a fort!"

"Oh, that's scary," Kenny said. "Where would we live then?"

"Maybe we can live in his old shoeboxes," I said. "There must be a thousand of them somewhere."

"Mikey," Kenny said. "There's just one problem with your fort idea. We build forts in your room. If he buys your house, you won't

HAVE a room."

"Ugh! Good point, Kenny. We have to build a fort outside then," I answered.

"On your front lawn?" he asked.

"Yes!" I said.

So, we did it. My parents were on the patio in the backyard talking and reading the newspaper, so they didn't hear or see us. It didn't take very long to bring a bunch of sofa and bed pillows out onto the front lawn and make an awesome fort with all kinds of secret passages.

I took an old plastic sword from a Halloween costume my brother wore a couple of years ago and stood in front of the fort. Sure enough, a little while later, Zeke and his parents took a walk past our house. They were smiling, but I knew they were rich and EVIL so I waved the sword and screamed, "You shall not pass!"

Zeke's parents both laughed and waved at me. They were power-walking which I really can't stand to look at because it gives me funny feelings. I overheard his mother say, "That Michael McMichaels really is a hoot!"

"Ok, you're not supposed to laugh!" I yelled at them. "I'm supposed to be scary!"

"Sure," they all said as they power–walked right past me.

A minute later I felt a tap on my shoulder. It was my mother's fingernail, I knew it.

"What on EARTH are you doing?" she said.

"I... ah... Kenny and I are... ah..." I couldn't tell her the real reason.

"You have lost your mind, Michael, it's official," my mom said. "Take all of my pillows back into the house this instant and wipe them off. There may be bugs on them now. How disgusting!"

"I'm sorry, Ma. We were just playing around," I tried to convince her.

Kenny and I spent the next hour cleaning up. I was glad she didn't punish me and that I could still bring Absimil to the county fair on Saturday.

"That's the last time I'll be seeing any of my furniture on the front lawn, ok, young man?" my mother added.

"OK, Ma, ok," I said.

Chapter 8

On Saturday morning, **I woke UP** and ran to the window. It was sunny and warm out. Perfect weather for the county fair. Absimil's parents had agreed to let him spend the day with us, and I was excited to show him around. There are all kinds of interesting things to do there, and, like my brother said, there is a contest with a big prize at the end of the day. This year I decided I HAD to win because I wanted to give the prize to my parents so we could afford to keep our house and not have to sell it to Zeke's family.

When we got to the fair, my mother told us to not wander too far off. There were thousands and thousands of happy people there, and I wished every day could be like that. You could smell hot-dogs and hamburgers on the grill and hear music from the stages by the side of the race track.

We arrived at the game where you shoot water into a clown's mouth and a balloon over his head fills up with air and finally pops. That's my favorite game so I asked my mother if we could play. She said yes.

Absimil seemed really excited, and he sat right next to me as we began to play.

"One, two, three," the girl who worked there shouted, and we began.

I closed one eye and was concentrating really hard when I saw Zeke and his family in the reflection in the mirror behind the clowns' heads.

"UGH!" I screamed, and then I lost control and started shooting water wildly all over the place. The employee tried to calm me down, but it wouldn't work because I was so nervous.

When the game was over, Absimil patted me on the back and told me not to worry, but he was laughing and he asked what happened.

"I… ah… got a bit distracted because I saw… a bee, and I was nervous that it would sting me," I explained.

Some old lady won the contest, but it didn't matter. I was more focused on the big prize of the night, which we discovered was a riddle contest. Whoever answered the most riddles correctly would win $200! I just discovered riddles recently when my uncle Anthony read me the book, *The Hobbit*. I thought I had a good chance of winning, but that contest was at the end of the night, after dinner and the concert, and there was a lot to do before then.

For example, there was a haunted house, and Absimil and I ran to wait in line for that. My parents and my sister waited off on the side. My brother met up with some friends and my parents let him spend a couple of hours with them.

While we were in line, I saw the back of a girl's head that looked familiar to me. I couldn't place it, but I knew it was familiar. Then I heard the voice say, in that English accent, "You know, one day I will be a princess because I will marry Prince

Harry and I will live in a castle – in several castles, you know, because the royal family is very, very rich, but none of you can visit me, I'm sad to say, because you are too American and common. I'm quite sorry, but it's true."

It was Harriet! Why couldn't I escape that girl and her annoying ways, even for just one day? **UGH!**

Just then, she turned around, saw me in the line behind her, and made that lizard face she's so good at by sticking out her tongue really fast.

I stuck out my tongue back at her and that was that.

Let me tell you, this was the scariest haunted house I have ever seen! It was **HUGE** and dark and there were all kinds of ghosts and goblins running around the place, scaring you half to death.

Absimil and I tried to pretend we weren't scared, but we were terrified.

We walked into a room that looked normal, with a sofa and a TV and all, but when we sat down, monsters jumped out from under the cushions under our butts, and we screamed and ran.

We were in a dark hallway, feeling our way with our hands, when all of a sudden a flashlight turned on right under the chin of a monster. Only it wasn't a monster, it was Zeke!

"OOOOOHHHHHHH!" he cried.

"Nice try, rich boy, but I'm not scared of you," I said.

Then he turned off the light and reached out for me in the darkness. It turns out I realized I WAS scared of him, so I screamed and grabbed Absimil's hand.

"Let's get out of here," I said, dragging him behind me.

We ran and ran in the darkness until we reached a door. I kicked it open and ran into the sunlight where I saw a bunch of people waiting in line for the ride. It was over and we were safe, phew! I looked over at Absimil and smiled for a second. Then I realized it was Harriet whose hand I had grabbed and pulled with me all that way.

Everyone outside was clapping at us as we stood there on the balcony looking down, still holding hands.

"Look! Romeo and Juliet!" one of the sixth graders in my school said.

"No, no, no," Harriet said, letting go of my hand. **"I would like to declare right now that I am betrothed – that**

means engaged to be married – to Prince Harry of England, not Michael McMichaels of America. **NO, NO, NO!"**

But everyone ignored her as usual, probably since they know Prince Harry is taken, and I made a lizard tongue at her again and walked away. I saw Absimil standing off on the side, and he was laughing, but I had to admit, it was kind of funny. I would be laughing, too, if he was holding Harriet's hand.

Chapter 9

Dinner at the fair was awesome: pizza and soda and nachos with cheese. Absimil had never eaten those things before, and it was great to watch his face as he bit into and tasted them for the first time. I wished I could speak his language because then, maybe, he'd open up more with me, but we're still getting to know each other, so it's not a problem.

After dinner, there was a concert that didn't last too long, but I got curious because a song the band sang was called 'God Bless the USA.' There was a line in it that confused me. It was, 'And I'm proud to be an American, where at least I know I'm free.'

That song made we wonder about Absimil. He's from Somalia and, as a refugee, he's not American yet.

"Mom," I said in a whisper so Absimil couldn't hear, "why did he say Americans are free? Does that mean other people from other countries are expensive?"

My mother laughed. "No," she said. "That has nothing to do with price or cost, it has to do with freedom and liberty."

"What kind of freedoms do we have?" I asked.

"Freedom to say what you want," she said. "To practice the religion you choose, to own property, and to determine what you want to be and do in your life."

"Oh," I said. "Does that include the freedom to be mean?"

"Well, I don't think that's what is meant by freedom," she said. "But if someone wants to be mean, you can just choose not to associate with that person anymore. That's a freedom, I suppose."

"Ok, so, is it bad not being an American?" I asked.

"No. People are born where they are born,

and it doesn't mean they are good or bad," she said. "You are a good or bad person based on what you do and how you treat other people. There are plenty of good and bad Americans, just as there are plenty of good and bad people from every country."

"Ok, but is it bad to say that a person is poor?" I asked.

"Well, how much money people have is just a fact about them, like their eye color or height," she said. "Besides, no one needs to be told how much money they have or don't have. If there's one thing people know, it's that! I don't see the need to remind them."

"Ok, thanks, Mom," I said.

After the concert was the riddle contest. I was psyched! There were 10 of us in the first round. Harriet had to drop out after the third round because she drank so much iced tea that she had to use the bathroom, and it was pretty far away. First, she did the bathroom dance for a few minutes. (You know, the one where you kind of hop up and down on one foot then the other and make all kinds of crazy faces?) Then she just ran for the bathroom and was out of the contest. After another two rounds, the kid division was now down to two: me and Zeke.

Just before the last riddle he leaned over to me and said, "Good luck, kid. I'm a pro at this.

I'll win the $200 and be even richer than I was yesterday!" But he seemed a bit nervous to me. I wondered why.

"Ok, we'll see. **Don't count your dollars before, uh, they hatch,**" I said.

"Dollars don't hatch," he said.

"I know! I started that but couldn't finish it," I admitted.

Then the old guy announcer asked the hardest riddle so far, "What is the quickest way of doubling your money?"

It was Zeke's turn to go first.

"By buying a house and selling it for more money. It's called flipping. There, I won. Yes! I won, right?" he said, hopping up and down like a kangaroo.

"No, that's not correct," the announcer said. "Now, it's your turn, Michael, and if you don't get it, you will both split the prize. Again, what is the quickest way of doubling your money? You have 30 seconds."

I began to sweat. **My heart was pounding** in my chest. I looked out at the crowd of my adoring fans, but nothing would come to me, nothing at all.

Then, suddenly I remembered seeing Zeke

and his family in that mirror when I was shooting the water into the clown's mouth. The thing is, I not only saw them, I saw MYSELF, or at least my reflection.

"I know," I cried, with three seconds left on the clock. "A mirror! A mirror is the quickest way of doubling your money!"

"Yes, that's right,"

the announcer said, and he shook my hand.

I looked over at Zeke, who was crying and rolling around on the floor like he was on fire. I was going to stick out my tongue at him, but he really looked so ridiculous that I decided it wasn't necessary. It was fun making a lizard tongue at Harriet every now and then because she was less crazy. I mean she acted crazy sometimes, for sure, but not like this.

No, this was different.

Chapter 10

At school on Monday morning, Kenny looked at me like something was wrong.

"Are you nervous, Mikey?" he asked.

"No, everything is fine," I said. But the truth was I was panicking because today is the deadline for me to call Absimil poor. If I can't do it, I'll lose the Double-Dog Dare contest, and that means Zeke is really Kenny's best friend.

"Ok. So, what did you do this weekend?" Kenny asked.

"I went to the county fair on Saturday with Absimil," I said. Just then Absimil walked by and waved to me. He was smiling.

"Oh," Kenny said. "Why didn't you invite me?"

"I forgot, I guess," I said. And it was true. I did forget. I was so focused on Absimil that I had forgotten all about Kenny.

"Well, no big deal," Kenny said, "We can go next year." But I could tell he was a bit upset, and it was my fault. I really should have invited him to go with us, only I got caught up in everything else. Sometimes life is difficult, but I really do try my best. Does that count for anything?

"Guess what, Kenny?" I said, remembering the money I had won. "I won $200 in the riddle contest."

"That's awesome! What are you going to buy with all that money?" he asked.

"Nothing," I said. "I'm going to stop Zeke from buying our house. That money-monkey is going to buy everyone's house in this whole town if we don't stop him soon."

I think Zeke could tell we were talking about him because he looked at me and mouthed the word, 'TODAY.' I knew that meant I had until the end of the day at school to complete the double-dog dare, but I had to wait for just the right time.

Just the right time came in the cafeteria. Kenny and I were sitting next to Absimil and, all of a sudden, Zeke plopped his tray down right beside us. He was making a mean face, and I knew why. I realized I had to end this now. An idea came to me.

"So, Absimil, you're not rich, right?" I asked. "Just like me and Kenny?"

"Yes," he said, taking a bite of his peanut butter and jelly sandwich. "We are poor, but we are happy."

"Ok, so you're poor but happy," I said, looking over at Zeke whose face was turning bright red. He assumed I would tell Absimil that he was poor in a nasty way, but I realized that it wasn't an insult after all, it was just a fact. Then I said to Zeke, "He's poor, I'm middle class, and you are rich. He's Somalian, we're American, and Prince Harry and Harriet are English. Everyone is different. What's the big deal?"

Then it happened: **Zeke LOST it.**

"You're poor!" he said to Absimil, jumping up onto the table. "You're poor and I'm rich! You're

83

POOOOORRRRRR!"

The whole cafeteria went silent. I looked over at Absimil, and he was shocked. It's a good thing that the lunch lady, Miss Fitzgerald, was standing right there. She insisted that Zeke stop shouting and get down from the table. She took him out of the cafeteria and, I guess, to Principal Stein's office.

I told Absimil not to worry, that Zeke was crazy, and most of the kids in our school were not like him.

"Thank you, Michael," he said. "We say in my language that all humans have faults. No one is perfect. Not me. Not Zeke. No one."

"That's so true, Absimil," I said.

"And, we are Somali not Somalian," he said, smiling.

"There you go! I have a fault, too!" I said.

Kenny leaned over and said, "Guess what, guys? I'm not perfect either. Sometimes I forget to flush the toilet and my whole family yells at me!"

Then we all laughed hard, which we really needed. I knew that that would be the end of the Double-Dog Dare contest even though it was technically my turn to dare Zeke.

On the bus on the way home, I told Kenny the whole story of the double-dog dares and that I thought he'd be Zeke's new best friend.

"You are truly nuts, Michael," he said. "I barely know that kid and you know I don't care how much money you have! Besides, he's too competitive for me. You've been my best friend for years."

"Yeah, and sorry again for not inviting you to the county fair," I said. "I got all caught up in this dare contest and I forgot."

"It's ok, Mikey," Kenny said.

"Thanks, Kenny!" Then I smiled and said, "But wait a second – you're saying that Zeke is too competitive – so does that make me a loooooser?"

"And UUUGLY!" he said, with a smile on his face.

"And smelly?" I asked with my nose scrunched up.

"And duuumb!" he kept piling it on.

"And have the cooties?" I just couldn't stop.

And we kept going until we laughed so hard the bus monitor told us to shush.

Chapter 11

As I expected, I was called to **Principal Stein's office** the next day. **Zeke was sitting there crying.**

"Michael, Zeke told me about the Double-Dog Dare contest you two engaged in," Principal Stein said. "Do you think things got out of hand?"

"Yes, Mr. Stein," I answered. "Things definitely got out of hand. But I was scared that he would be able to say he was Kenny's best friend and also that he would buy our house because he's so rich and keeps buying everything he sees."

Mr. Stein explained that Zeke couldn't buy our house unless we wanted to sell it, even if he had all the money in the world. I didn't know that little fact. Oops! He also told me that if I was afraid of losing Kenny as a friend, I should have spoken to Kenny directly about it. Then he told me he didn't want to hear again of any more Double-Dog Dare contests. He also said it was rude of us to embarrass Harriet in class the other day with the proposal and, of course, we should never comment on anyone being poor. It's mean. And it's not behavior he would tolerate.

We both agreed.

On the way out of his office, I saw Zeke's parents arrive. I'm sure they were going to hear all about the incident in the cafeteria as well as our Double-Dog Dare contest.

Later that day, Ms. Mitchell surprised all of us by saying she wanted to tell us something. Everyone was silent, sitting on the rug we used for story time.

"You all know what happened yesterday in the cafeteria," she said. Zeke lowered his head, but he was still listening, I could tell. "I'm not going to scold anyone now because Mr. Stein did that yesterday. I want to talk to all of you about what is appropriate to say to other people if you want to be a kind, decent person, which is my goal for all of you inside this classroom and outside as well. We are all, of course, different but we have many things in common. It is natural to be curious about certain things and as long as you ask politely, most of the time it will not come across badly. However, pointing out certain things that don't need to be said is simply mean and unnecessary."

Just then everyone looked at Zeke. He was looking at the ground and covering his eyes.

"But," Ms. Mitchell continued, "we all make mistakes and deserve to be forgiven if we are truly sorry."

"Even Zeke?" Harriet asked. I'm glad she asked that. I was wondering it. We probably all were.

"Yes, Harriet, even Zeke," she said. "He has apologized to Absimil for his outburst and has promised to not do such a thing again. Again, we all make mistakes. Let's not forget that. All of us. The key thing is that we acknowledge these errors, apologize for them, and promise to be better in the future."

"Ms. Mitchell, Absimil said that in his language there is a saying about making mistakes," I said.

"Really, Absimil? Can we hear it in your language?" she asked.

Absimil smiled, stood up, and said the words which seemed to flow perfectly and were very beautiful to hear.

We all tried to repeat it and he giggled the first few times. Apparently, we sounded terrible! But after a few tries we got better, because eventually we learned from our mistakes.

Chapter 12

A few weeks later, Zeke's family wound up moving out of the neighborhood because the bank took both of their houses from them. I asked my mother why the bank would do that if they were so rich. She said they weren't actually that rich. They bought most things on credit cards and couldn't keep up with the payments. Now it made sense to me why he was so obsessed with money and calling people poor – because he knew that was his family's problem, or would soon be. He was upset he lost the riddle contest because he really needed the $200 to help his family.

Absimil moved, too, to another state where some of his relatives lived. His father got a job at a university as a scientist and his family was excited for this new step.

"Mom," I said over breakfast (pancakes and bacon – my favorite!), "what do you think will happen to Zeke and his family? Will they be homeless?"

"I don't know, Michael," she said. "Last I heard they were moving in with Zeke's mother's family near Atlanta."

"I have an idea,"

I said. "How about I give Zeke's family some of the riddle contest money I won last month?"

"That would be very nice of you, Michael," she replied.

"Yeah, I'll give them a $100 and keep the rest, I think. But, I also owe Mr. Jacobs $5, and a few of our other neighbors some more money, so I need to pay them, too." Then I explained that I owed them the money because I had collected to help save our house. My mother was not pleased, but she said she understood given the circumstances.

"Sounds like a plan," my mother said. "And don't forget to apologize to each and every one of them, too, when you pay them back. It's wrong to have asked for money, saying you were going to give it to the poor."

"Ok, I understand," I said. "And, Ma, can I have some of the money so Kenny and I can play games at the arcade. I forgot to ask him to go to the county fair, and I owe him a favor now."

"Sure, Michael. Why don't you call him and see if he's free this afternoon? I have to go to the mall to run some errands anyway," she said.

I called. Kenny said he was free and would love to come to the arcade with me. **I smiled because it's always fun spending time with my best friend.**

Tips & Questions

"I got really depressed that I would lose the bet and that would mean Kenny is not my best friend anymore." - Michael McMichaels

"I want to talk to all of you about what is appropriate to say to other people if you want to be a kind, decent person, which is my goal for all of you inside this classroom and outside as well. We are all, of course, different but we have many things in common. It is natural to be curious about certain things and as long as you ask politely, most of the time it will not come across badly. However, pointing out certain things that don't need to be said is simply mean and unnecessary."

– Ms. Mitchell

1. **ASK -** Who is your best friend? How long have you been friends? Why is this person so special to you? What are his/her best qualities? Were you ever scared of losing him/her as a friend? What happened?

2. **ASK -** What is the best birthday gift you ever received? Who gave it to you? Why was it so special? What is the best gift you ever gave? What made it so special?

3. **DISCUSS -** Why is it important not to judge people based on the amount of money they have? How should a person's true worth be measured?

4. **DISCUSS** – What are examples of fun contests that friends can compete in that don't result in hurting other people's feelings?

5. **SHARE** – Think of an instance in your life when you felt the pressure to compete for something. What was it? What did you do to try to achieve it? Did you get carried away like Michael did in this book?

6. **DISCUSS** – What does it mean to be jealous of someone? How can jealousy be a bad thing?

7. **SHARE** – Talk about a time in your life when you were jealous of someone. What did you do to overcome it?

8. **DISCUSS** – Michael's neighbor, Mr. Jacobs, tells Michael and his sister, "It's better to be humble and modest like your family." What does he mean by that? Do you agree? Why or why not?

9. **CONSIDER** – Parents and teachers, what can you do to help create an environment where children can learn to be content with what they have? What strategies can you provide children with to cope with jealousy when it arises?

Boys Town Press Featured Titles

Kid-friendly books to teach social skills

978-1-934490-66-2

978-1-934490-79-2

978-1-944882-06-8

978-1-934490-92-1

978-1-944882-10-5

978-1-944882-03-7

978-1-934490-94-5

978-1-934490-54-9

978-1-934490-60-0

978-1-934490-87-7

978-1-934490-77-8

BoysTownPress.org

For information on Boys Town, its Education Model®, Common Sense Parenting®, and training programs:
boystowntraining.org , boystown.org/parenting
EMAIL: training@BoysTown.org, PHONE: 1-800-545-5771

For parenting and educational books and other resources:
BoysTownPress.org, EMAIL: btpress@BoysTown.org, PHONE: 1-800-282-6657